BELPHAGOR

Belphagor

NICCOLO MACHIAVELLI

ILLUSTRATED BY DANUTA LASKOWSKA

MINIATURE BOOKS · RODALE PRESS

FIRST PUBLISHED IN THIS EDITION 1954
BY THE RODALE PRESS
EMMAUS, PENNSYLVANIA AND
123 NEW BOND STREET, LONDON, ENGLAND
MANUFACTURED IN ENGLAND

PREFACE

THE NAME OF MACHIAVELLI HAS BECOME so closely identified with his great work of political analysis *The Prince* that many of us can place him only as a dark Renaissance figure 'destitute of political morality, following expediency rather than right, cunning, crafty, perfidious' — for so the dictionary defines the adjective 'Machiavellian'.

Niccolò Machiavelli was in fact the least Machiavellian of men. A true child of the Renaissance (he was born in Florence in 1469 and died there in 1527) he could turn his hand to many things. A conscientious and very capable civil servant by profession, he was the author of numerous volumes of history and political theory, a dramatist of distinction and even the composer of popular songs for singing in the streets at carnival time.

It is of course on *The Prince* that Machiavelli's fame rests. The book is a study of 'the art of government' for the guidance of the autocratic sovereign. The end Machiavelli sets before his Prince is the strong, prosperous, peaceful State, united under the rule of a father of his people, and able to call on the services of its own citizens for its own defence. It is the means he advocates to attain this end which have made his book the subject of violent dispute for over four centuries. To preserve the well-being of the State the Prince can resort to any treachery, dissimulation, deception or violence, for, says Machiavelli, 'the generality of mankind are wicked and ever ready to break their words'. The advice is not by any means as cynical as it sounds when we remember that Machiavelli lived in the age of the Borgias, the Orsini, and the Sforzas. To survive in this company a ruler had to poison before he was poisoned, stab before he was stabbed, and bribe his enemy's mercenary troops to desert before his own received the same treatment.

Machiavelli saw the political facts of life as they were. He had considerable experi-

ence of them. For thirteen years as Secretary
to the Second Chancery, one of the govern-
ing bodies of Florence, he negotiated with
such formidable figures as Cesare Borgia,
Caterina Sforza, Louis XII of France, the
lecherous Pope Alexander, and the warrior
Pope Julius. He lost this post on the return
of the Medici to Florence and it was during
the years in the wilderness which followed
that a great part of his writing was done.
The Prince was finished in 1513 and it
seems probable that *Belphagor* was written
within the next three or four years, possibly
as a relief from the histories.

This little novella is full of the sturdy
humour of the Renaissance. It takes as its
theme the hell of the unhappily married and
Macaulay suggested that Machiavelli's wife
Marietta was the inspiration for the story;
but later biographers have stoutly denied
that Niccolò and Marietta were anything
but the most devoted couple in spite of the
many lapses from the strictest fidelity
recorded in his letters.

Belphagor

WE READ IN THE ANCIENT ARCHIVES OF Florence the following account, as it was received from the lips of a very holy man, greatly respected by every one for the sanctity of his manners at the period in which he lived. Happening once to be deeply absorbed in his prayers, such was their efficacy that he saw an infinite number of condemned souls, belonging to those miserable mortals who had died in their sins, undergoing the punishment due to their offences in the regions below. He remarked that the greater part of them lamented nothing so bitterly as their folly in having taken wives, attributing to them the whole of their misfortunes. Much surprised at this, Minos and Rhadamanthus, with the rest of the infernal judges, unwilling to credit all the abuse heaped upon the female sex, and wearied from day to day with its repetition, agreed to bring the matter before Pluto. It was then resolved that the conclave of infernal princes should form a committee of inquiry, and should adopt such measures as might be deemed most advisable by the court in order to discover the truth or falsehood of the calumnies which they heard.

All being assembled in council, Pluto addressed them as follows: 'Dearly beloved demons! Though by celestial dispensation and the irreversible decree of fate this kingdom fell to my share, and I might strictly dispense with any kind of celestial or earthly responsibility, yet, as it is more prudent and respectful to consult the laws and to hear the opinion of others, I have resolved to be guided by your advice, particularly in a case that may chance to cast some imputation upon our government. For the souls of all men daily arriving in our kingdom still continue to lay the whole blame upon their wives, and as this appears to us impossible, we must be careful how we decide in such a business, lest we also should come in for a share of their abuse,

on account of our too great severity; and yet judgement must be pronounced, lest we be taxed with negligence and with indifference to the interests of justice.

'Now, as the latter is the fault of a careless, and the former of an unjust judge, we, wishing to avoid the trouble and the blame that might attach to both, yet hardly seeing how to get clear of it, naturally enough apply to you for assistance, in order that you may look to it, and contrive in some way that, as we have hitherto reigned without the slightest imputation upon our character, we may continue to do so for the future.'

The affair appearing to be of the utmost importance to all the princes present, they first resolved that it was necessary to ascertain the truth, though they differed as to the best means of accomplishing this object. Some were of opinion that they ought to choose one or more from among themselves, who should be commissioned to pay a visit to the world, and in a human shape endeavour personally to ascertain how far such reports were grounded in truth. To many others it appeared that this might be done without so much trouble merely by compelling some of the wretched souls to confess the truth by the application of a variety of tortures. But the majority being in favour of a journey to the world, they abided by the former proposal. No one, however, being ambitious of undertaking such a task, it was resolved to leave the affair to chance. The lot fell upon the arch-devil Belphagor, who, previous to the Fall, had enjoyed the rank of archangel in a higher world. Though he received his commission with a very ill grace, he nevertheless felt himself constrained by Pluto's imperial mandate, and prepared to execute whatever had been determined upon in council. At the same time he took an oath to observe the tenor of his instructions, as they had been drawn up with all due solemnity and ceremony for the purpose of his mission.

These were to the following effect:— *Imprimis*, that the better to promote the object in view, he should be furnished with a hundred thousand gold ducats; secondly, that he should make use of the utmost expedition in getting into the world; thirdly, that after assuming the human form he should enter into the marriage state; and lastly, that he should live with his wife for the space of ten years. At the expiration of this period, he was to feign death and return home, in order to acquaint his employers, by the fruits of experience, what really were the respective conveniences and inconveniences of matrimony. The conditions further ran, that during the said ten years he should be subject to all kinds of miseries and disasters, like the rest of mankind, such as poverty, prisons, and diseases into which men are apt to fall, unless, indeed, he could contrive by his own skill and ingenuity to avoid them.

Poor Belphagor having signed these conditions and received the money, forthwith came into the world, and having set up his equipage, with a numerous train of servants, he made a very splendid entrance into Florence. He selected this city in preference to all others, as being most favourable for obtaining an usurious interest of his money; and having assumed the name of Roderigo, a native of Castile, he took a house in the suburbs of Ognissanti. And because he was unable to explain the instructions under which he acted, he gave out that he was a merchant, who having had poor prospects in Spain, had gone to Syria, and succeeded in acquiring his fortune at Aleppo, whence he had lastly set out for Italy, with the intention of marrying and settling there, as one of the most polished and agreeable countries he knew.

Roderigo was certainly a very handsome man, apparently about thirty years of age, and he lived in a style of life that showed he was in pretty easy circumstances, if not possessed of immense wealth. Being, moreover, extremely affable and liberal, he soon attracted the notice of many noble citizens blessed with large families of daughters and small incomes. The former of these were soon offered to him, from among whom Roderigo chose a very beautiful girl of the name of Onesta, a daughter of Amerigo Donati, who had also three sons, all grown up, and three more daughters, also nearly marriageable. Though of a noble family and enjoying a good reputation in Florence, his father-in-law was extremely poor, and maintained as poor an establishment. Roderigo, therefore, made very splendid nuptials, and omitted nothing that might tend to confer honour upon such a festival, being liable, under the law which he received on leaving his infernal abode, to feel all kinds of vain and earthly passions.

He therefore soon began to enter into all the pomps and vanities of the world, and to aim at reputation and consideration among mankind, which put him to no little expense. But more than this, he had not long enjoyed the society of his beloved Onesta, before he became tenderly attached

to her, and was unable to behold her suffer the slightest inquietude or vexation. Now, along with her other gifts of beauty and nobility, the lady had brought into the house of Roderigo such an insufferable portion of pride, that in this respect Lucifer himself could not equal her; for her husband, who had experienced the effects of both, was at no loss to decide which was the more intolerable of the two. Yet it became infinitely worse when she discovered the extent of Roderigo's attachment to her, of which she availed herself to obtain an ascendancy over him and rule him with a rod of iron. Not content with this, when she found he would bear it, she continued to annoy him with all kinds of insults and taunts, in such a way as to give him the most indescribable pain and uneasiness. For what with the influence of her father, her brothers, her friends, and relatives, the duty of the matrimonial yoke, and the love he bore her, he suffered all for some time with the patience of a saint.

It would be useless to recount the follies and extravagancies into which he ran in order to gratify her taste for dress, and

every article of the newest fashion, in which
our city, ever so variable in its nature,
according to its usual habits, so much
abounds. Yet, to live upon easy terms with
her, he was obliged to do more than this;
he had to assist his father-in-law in por-
tioning off his other daughters; and she next
asked him to furnish one of her brothers
with goods to sail for the Levant, another
with silks for the West, while a third was
to be set up in a goldbeater's establishment
at Florence. In such objects the greatest
part of his fortune was soon consumed.

At length the Carnival season was at
hand; the festival of St. John was to be
celebrated, and the whole city, as usual,
was in a ferment. Numbers of the noblest
families were about to vie with each other
in the splendour of their parties, and the
Lady Onesta, being resolved not to be out-
shone by her acquaintance, insisted that
Roderigo should exceed them all in the
richness of their feasts. For the reasons
above stated, he submitted to her will; nor,
indeed, would he have scrupled at doing
much more, however difficult it might have
been, could he have flattered himself with

a hope of preserving the peace and comfort of his household, and of awaiting quietly the consummation of his ruin. But this was not the case, inasmuch as the arrogant temper of his wife had grown to such a height of asperity by long indulgence, that he was at a loss in what way to act. His domestics, male and female, would no longer remain in the house, being unable to support for any length of time the intolerable life they led. The inconvenience which he suffered in consequence of having no one to whom he could entrust his affairs it is impossible to express. Even his own familiar devils, whom he had brought along with him, had already deserted him, choosing to return below rather than submit longer to the tyranny of his wife.

Left, then, to himself, amidst this turbulent and unhappy life, and having dissipated all the ready money he possessed, he was compelled to live upon the hopes of the returns expected from his ventures in the East and the West. Being still in good credit, in order to support his rank he resorted to bills of exchange; nor was it long before, accounts running against him, he found himself in the same situation as many other unhappy speculators in that market. Just as his case became extremely delicate, there arrived sudden tidings both from East and West that one of his wife's brothers had dissipated the whole of Roderigo's profits in play, and that while the other was returning with a rich cargo uninsured, his ship had the misfortune to be wrecked, and he himself was lost. No sooner did this affair transpire than his creditors assembled, and supposing it must be all over with him, though their bills had not yet become due, they resolved to keep a strict watch over him in fear that he might abscond.

Roderigo, on his part, thinking that there was no other remedy, and feeling how deeply he was bound by the Stygian law, determined at all hazards to make his escape. So taking horse one morning early, as he luckily lived near the Prato gate, in that direction he went off. His departure was soon known; the creditors were all in a bustle; the magistrates were applied to, and the officers of justice, along with a great part of the populace, were despatched in pursuit.

Roderigo had hardly proceeded a mile
before he heard this hue and cry, and the
pursuers were soon so close at his heels
that the only resource he had left was to
abandon the highroad and take to the open
country, with the hope of concealing himself in the fields. But finding himself unable
to make way over the hedges and ditches,
he left his horse and took to his heels,
traversing fields of vines and canes, until
he reached Peretola, where he entered the
house of Matteo del Bricca, a labourer of
Giovanna del Bene. Finding him at home,

for he was busily providing fodder for his cattle, our hero earnestly entreated him to save him from the hands of his adversaries close behind, who would infallibly starve him to death in a dungeon, engaging that if Matteo would give him refuge, he would make him one of the richest men alive, and afford him such proofs of it before he took his leave as would convince him of the truth of what he said; and if he failed to do this, he was quite content that Matteo himself should deliver him into the hands of his enemies.

Now Matteo, although a rustic, was a man of courage, and concluding that he could not lose anything by the speculation, he gave him his hand and agreed to save him. He then thrust our hero under a heap of rubbish, completely enveloping him in weeds; so that when his pursuers arrived they found themselves quite at a loss, nor could they extract from Matteo the least information as to his appearance. In this dilemma there was nothing left for them but to proceed in the pursuit, which they continued for two days, and then returned, jaded and disappointed, to Florence. In the meanwhile, Matteo drew our hero from his hiding-place, and begged him to fulfil his engagement.

To this his friend Roderigo replied: 'I confess, brother, that I am under great obligations to you, and I mean to return them. To leave no doubt upon your mind, I will inform you who I am'; and he proceeded to acquaint him with all the particulars of the affair; how he had come into the world, and married, and run away. He next described to his preserver the way in which he might become rich, which was briefly as follows. As soon as Matteo should hear of some lady in the neighbourhood being said to be possessed, he was to conclude that it was Roderigo himself who had taken possession of her; and he gave him his word, at the same time, that he would never leave her until Matteo should come and conjure him to depart. In this way he might obtain what sum he pleased from the lady's friends for the price of exorcising her; and having mutually agreed upon this plan, Roderigo disappeared.

Not many days elapsed before it was reported in Florence that the daughter of

Messer Ambrogio Amedei, a lady married to Buonajuto Tebalducci, was possessed by the devil. Her relations did not fail to apply every means usual on such occasions to expel him, such as making her wear upon her head St. Zanobi's cap, and the cloak of St. John of Gualberto; but these had only the effect of making Roderigo laugh. And to convince them that it was really a spirit that possessed her, and that it was no flight of the imagination, he made the young lady talk Latin, hold a philosophical dispute, and reveal the frailties of many of her acquaintance. He particularly accused a certain friar of having introduced a lady into his monastery in male attire, to the no small scandal of all who heard it, and the astonishment of the brotherhood. Messer Ambrogio found it impossible to silence him, and began to despair of his daughter's cure.

But the news reaching Matteo, he lost no time in waiting upon Ambrogio, assuring him of his daughter's recovery on condition of his paying him five hundred florins, with which to purchase a farm at Peretola. To this Messer Ambrogio consented; and

Matteo immediately ordered a number of masses to be said, after which he proceeded with some unmeaning ceremonies calculated to give solemnity to his task. Then approaching the young lady, he whispered in her ear: 'Roderigo, it is Matteo that is come. So do as we agreed upon, and get out.' Roderigo replied: 'It is all well; but you have not asked enough to make you a rich man. So when I depart I will take possession of the daughter of Charles, King of Naples, and I will not leave her till you come. You may then demand whatever you please for your reward; and mind that you never trouble me again.' And when he had said this, he went out of the lady, to the no small delight and amazement of the whole city of Florence.

It was not long again before the accident that had happened to the daughter of the King of Naples began to be buzzed about the country, and all the monkish remedies having been found to fail, the king, hearing of Matteo, sent for him from Florence.

On arriving at Naples, Matteo, after a few ceremonies, performed the cure. Before leaving the princess, however, Roderigo said: 'You see, Matteo, I have kept my promise and made a rich man of you, and I owe you nothing now. So, henceforward you will take care to keep out of my way, lest as I have hitherto done you some good, just the contrary should happen to you in future.' Upon this Matteo thought it best to return to Florence, after receiving fifty thousand ducats from His Majesty, in order to enjoy his riches in peace, and never once imagined that Roderigo would come in his way again. But in this he was deceived; for he soon heard that a daughter of Louis, King of France, was possessed by an evil spirit, which disturbed our friend Matteo not a little, thinking of His Majesty's great authority and of what Roderigo had said.

Hearing of Matteo's great skill, and finding no other remedy, the king despatched a messenger for him, whom Matteo contrived to send back with a variety of excuses. But this did not long avail him; the king applied to the Florentine council, and our hero was compelled to attend. Arriving with no very pleasant sensations at Paris, he was introduced into the royal presence, when he assured His Majesty that though it was true he had acquired some fame in the course of his demoniac practice, he could by no means always boast of success, and that some devils were of such a desperate character as not to pay the least attention to threats, enchantments, or even the exorcisms of religion itself. He would, nevertheless, do His Majesty's pleasure, entreating at the same time to be held excused if it should happen to prove an obstinate case. To this the king made answer, that be the case what it might, he would certainly hang him if he did not succeed.

It is impossible to describe poor Matteo's terror and perplexity on hearing these words; but at length mustering courage, he ordered the possessed princess to be brought into his presence. Approaching as usual close to her ear, he conjured Roderigo in the most humble terms, by all he had ever done for him, not to abandon him in such a dilemma, but to show some sense of gratitude for past services and to leave the princess. 'Ah! thou traitorous villain!' cried Roderigo, 'hast thou, indeed, ventured to meddle in this business? Dost thou

boast thyself a rich man at my expense?
I will now convince the world and thee of
the extent of my power, both to give and to
take away. I shall have the pleasure of
seeing thee hanged before thou leavest this
place.'

Poor Matteo finding there was no
remedy, said nothing more, but, like a wise
man, set his head to work in order to discover some other means of expelling the
spirit; for which purpose he said to the
king, 'Sire, it is as I feared: there are certain
spirits of so malignant a character that
there is no keeping any terms with them,
and this is one of them. However, I will
make a last attempt, and I trust that it will
succeed according to our wishes. If not,
I am in Your Majesty's power, and I hope
you will take compassion on my innocence.
In the first place, I have to entreat that
Your Majesty will order a large stage to be
erected in the centre of the great square,
such as will admit the nobility and clergy
of the whole city. The stage ought to be
adorned with all kinds of silks and with
cloth of gold, and with an altar raised in the
middle. To-morrow morning I would have

Your Majesty, with your full train of lords and ecclesiastics in attendance, seated in order and in magnificent array, as spectators of the scene at the said place. There, after having celebrated solemn mass, the possessed princess must appear; but I have in particular to entreat that on one side of the square may be stationed a band of men with drums, trumpets, horns, tambours, bagpipes, cymbals, and kettledrums, and all other kinds of instruments that make the most infernal noise. Now, when I take my hat off, let the whole band strike up, and approach with the most horrid uproar towards the stage. This, along with a few other secret remedies which I shall apply, will surely compel the spirit to depart.'

These preparations were accordingly made by the royal command; and when the day, being Sunday morning, arrived, the stage was seen crowded with people of rank and the square with the people. Mass was celebrated, and the possessed princess conducted between two bishops, with a train of nobles, to the spot.

Now, when Roderigo beheld so vast a concourse of people, together with all this awful preparation, he was almost struck dumb with astonishment, and said to himself, 'I wonder what that cowardly wretch is thinking of doing now? Does he imagine I have never seen finer things than these in the regions above—ay! and more horrid things below! However, I will soon make him repent it, at all events.' Matteo then approaching him, besought him to come out; but Roderigo replied, 'Oh, you think you have done a fine thing now! What do you mean to do with all this trumpery? Can you escape my power, think you, in this way, or elude the vengeance of the king? Thou poltroon villain, I will have thee hanged for this!'

And as Matteo continued the more to entreat him, his adversary still vilified him in the same strain. So Matteo, believing there was no time to be lost, made the sign with his hat, when all the musicians who had been stationed there for the purpose suddenly struck up a hideous din, and ringing a thousand peals, approached the spot. Roderigo pricked up his ears at the sound, quite at a loss what to think, and rather in a perturbed tone of voice he asked

Matteo what it meant. To this the latter returned, apparently much alarmed: 'Alas! dear Roderigo, it is your wife; she is coming for you!' It is impossible to give an idea of the anguish of Roderigo's mind and the strange alteration which his feelings underwent at that name. The moment the name of 'wife' was pronounced, he had no longer presence of mind to consider whether it were probable, or even possible, that it could be she. Without replying a single word, he leaped out and fled in the utmost terror, leaving the lady to herself, and preferring rather to return to his infernal abode and render an account of his adventures than run the risk of any further sufferings and vexations under the matrimonial yoke.

And thus Belphagor again made his appearance in the infernal domains, bearing ample testimony to the evils introduced into a household by a wife; while Matteo, on his part, who knew more of the matter than the devil, returned triumphantly home, not a little proud of the victory he had achieved.